W9-BIM-277

Pea, Bee, & Jay

FARM FEUD

Brian "Smitty" Smith

An Imprint of HarperCollinsPublishers

GRUMBLE
GRUMBLE
GRUMBLE
I can't believe you said that! Take it back at ONCE!

ME?!? YOU'RE the one who needs to apologize!

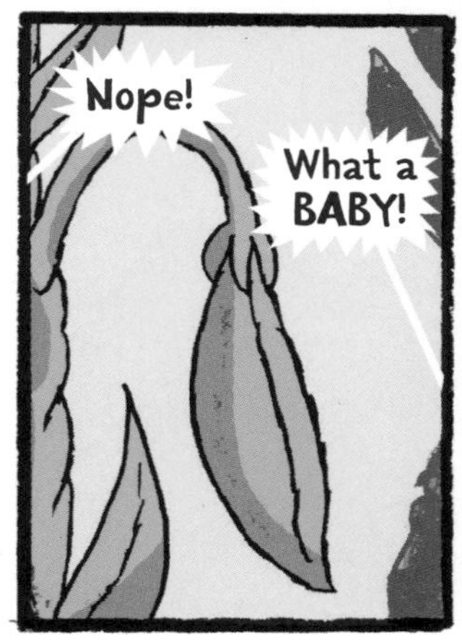
Nope!
What a BABY!

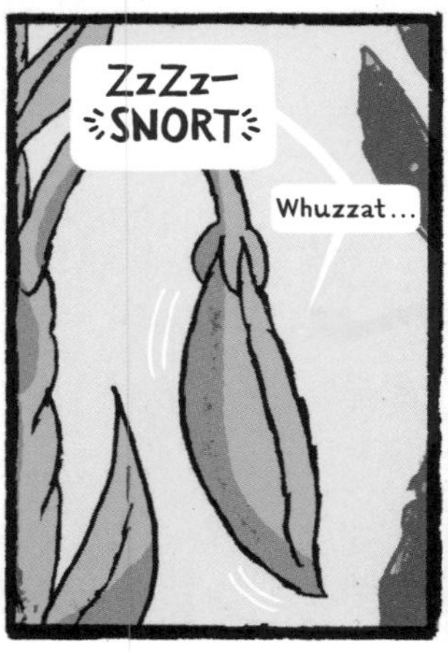
ZzZz— SNORT
Whuzzat...

Say that to my face!
I am!

GRUMBLE GRUMBLE GRUMBLE
Who in the name of VEGETATION is disturbing mah BEAUTY SLEEP?
YAWN GRAMPS?

What time is it?
Time to go kick some PEA-HINDS!

GRUMBLE GRUMBLE
I can't take it anymore! Somebody HARVEST me!
GRUMBLE GRUMBLE
Those two don't CARROT ALL about our rest.

GRUMBLE GRUMBLE GRUMBLE
All this noise is making me SQUIRM—and I don't even have EARS!

Ten-hut, acorns! We've received info about a disturbance on the FARM!

I need you to check it out, Private. Report back on any SUSPICIOUS ACTIVITY!
You got it, sir!

Do you guys wanna join my RAP GROUP?
Sounds LAME, Blue.
Yeah! Ask PEA, if he ever bothers to show up!

So long FOREVER, cocoon!

You are INFURIATING!
Uh...
No YOU are!

...on second thought, I think I'm better off in here.
SLAM

GRUMBLE
GRUMBLE
GRUMBLE
Sounds like a real brawl is about to break out!

LENNY! Have you seen our beloved QUEEN BEE this morning?
Relax, fellas. I'm sure she's just HAVING FUN with her friends.

They're even crabbier than us crab apples!
GRUMBLE
GRUMBLE
GRUMBLE
AH SHADAAAAP!

GRUMBLE
GRUMBLE
GRUMBLE
GRUMBLE
Those two are making a MOLEHILL out of an ANTHILL!
I'll say!

I'll give them PUMPKIN to complain about!
GRUMBLE
GRUMBLE
They're out of their GOURDS!
GRUMBLE

Now you've **REALLY** done it, **BEE!** I'm hoppin' mad!
Whatever, **PEA!**
I've never been **SO ANGRY** in my whole life!

YOU'RE the one who started it!
It was **YOU!**
Whoa, whoa, whoa! What's going on here?

It's all Bee's fault!

I DISAGREE!
It was Pea!

You believe ME, don't you Jay?
Nonsense! Jay is on MY side!
Right, Jay?
I'm so confused.

You can tell Pea that I'M not speaking to him!
And you can tell Bee that I'm not gonna talk to her EITHER!

Um...you can still HEAR each other, right?

Listen, Bee... we both know Pea can be a bit of a hothead...
That's no excuse to talk to me in that manner.
I'm ROYALTY!

You're a ROYAL PAIN, that's for sure!

You think you're so smart, don't ya?
I AM smart, you PEA BRAIN!

You take that back.
NEVER.
In fact, how about I take it UP a notch?

I challenge you to a duel!

I'm not afraid of your BUTT!
Get a good look at MY butt!
It's my STINGER!

Everyone put their butts away!
Here—let me show you what I made!

RUSTLE
RUSTLE
RUSTLE

It's a scale model of the whole farm built from twigs and leaves!
I figured we could use it to plan our adventures.

Not a chance!
That goes DOUBLE for me!
No adventures?!? This MUST be serious!
Could one of you PLEASE explain what you're arguing about?
Sure! I'm right and Bee's NOT.
Except the EXACT OPPOSITE!
Hmmm.
Seems to me that neither of you wants to admit you're wrong.

Bah! I'll go find some NEW FRIENDS who appreciate me!
No–Bee, wait!

Yeah, right! MY new friends are gonna be the COOLEST EVER!
Not you too, Pea!

COME BACK!!!

SIGH
Now I don't have any friends...

Ssssounds like you're better off.
Huh?

FLAP
Is somebody there?
Jussst a concerned passsserby.
I couldn't help but overhear your ssssituation.

Where are you?
Thisss way. In the grasssss.

Pea and Bee never fight like that.
I don't even know what they were fighting about!

Are you still here?
Yesssss.

Uh...
I hear you but I can't SEE you.

Isss thisss better?
Oh, yes. Much.
I'm Jay. Pleased to meet you!

My, you certainly are big.
Are you an elephant?
I am a SSSSNAKE.

Tell me . . .
what do you TASSSTE like?

I've never checked! Lemme see.
LICK LICK LICK
Like FEATHERS, I guess.

Would you sssay you are EASSSSY to DIGESSSST?
You sure ask some interesting questions, snake.

I'd love to stay and chat but I'm feeling bluer than ever.
I just lost my two best friends!
I sssee.

A SSSNUGGLE, perhapsss?

I'm sorry—that does sound nice but I really must be going.

BONK

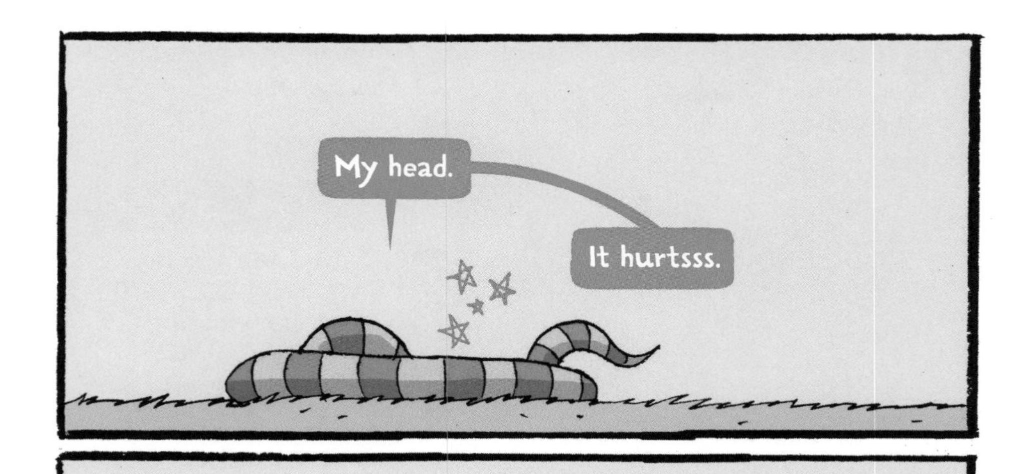
My head.
It hurtsss.

I have to help Bee and Pea patch things up...
They might disagree but they're BOTH wrong.
You can't just REPLACE your best friends. I wish there was some way I could MAKE them get along.
Wait— that's it!
Jay you're a GENIUS!

MEANWHILE...
This is gonna be SO MUCH FUN!
Just me and my TWO NEW BEST BUDS on an exciting ADVENTURE!

Ha! You know ol' Lenny. If there's one thing he loves, it's honey!
Uh-right! HONEY! Sure thing!
Honey?

I thought Pea said we were gonna start a RAP GROUP.
A RAP GROUP?
Ooh, wait'll Bee hears about this. She's gonna be sooo JEALOUS!
Yeah!

Pea told me he found a bunch of honey and we were going to go get it.
Hey! What's the holdup back there?

We're confused.
Come on you two! Pick up the pace!
VERY.

I gotta say, you two aren't showing much gratitude for being PERSONALLY invited to hang out with ME.
ESPECIALLY when I'm about to show you the COOLEST place on the FARM.

So, this sweet spot...
...how much honey are we talking here?
Is it a good place to form a RAP GROUP?
I really just want to BEATBOX.

NOW I see why you're confused.
What I said was "I found a SWEET SPOT for a GROUP of adventurers."

Now that we all understand each other, let's get moving!
This adventure isn't gonna adventure itself!

Ha-ha! I can't wait to see the look on Bee's face. It's gonna be priceless.

I think we've been tricked.
Sure looks that way.
Come on!

She's probably back at the hive moping around, wishing she was having fun like me!

Is that so?
Huh?

As you can plainly see, my new friends and I are having tons of fun!
We are?
Freeze, punks!

Well, well, well... SPYING on me, eh?
That's a pretty low move, Bee. Almost as low as stealing my Gramps!

How could you side with Bee instead of me?
Your momma said she needed some "me" time and paid Bee to take me for a long walk.
Ha! I knew it!
That's beside the point. What are YOU doing hanging out with Lenny?
He's one of MY loyal subjects!

There might have been a mixed message regarding some HONEY.
Sounds SUSPICIOUS to me.

As your Queen, I demand you get back to work at the hive this instant!
But it's my day off!

YOU!
You look like a troublemaker.
Empty your POCKETS!

I don't have any pockets.
Then YOU do it!
NO ONE HAS POCKETS!

That guy is INTENSE.
For reals!
Nice friend you've got there, Bee.
Looks like they all HID their pockets before we got here.
You're really not helping at all.

Gramps—tell them how much fun we've been having!

You never stop JIBBER-JABBERING and the other one keeps STARING at me all wild-eyed. The only fun I get to have is when you TALK ME to SLEEP.

Yep! That sounds about right.
YOU'RE not helping either!

C'mon pals. Let's get out of here and show those guys what having fun is all about.
Today is gonna be absolutely EPIC...
...like WAYYYY cooler than anything they're gonna do!
What's with the POCKETS?

An OBVIOUS overstatement from a HOTHEADED LOUDMOUTH.
WE'LL be the ones to maximize today's FUN ALLOTMENT!
Wait until you find out about all of the EXCITING THINGS I have planned next!

You're going to wish you apologized when you had the chance!
YOU'RE gonna wish YOU apologized!
Just stay out of OUR way!
YOU stay out of OUR way!
I can't hear you!
I can't hear you EITHER!

BACK AT THE NEST...
Let's see...

...this'll work...

...and some of THESE...

...throw in some of THOSE...

HUP!

...aaand BUILD!

Done!
I can't make my friends talk to each other...

...but I CAN make my friends!

Hey, Pea!
Why don't we start with a little rolling?
Wow! Look at you go!

THWAP

Oh my!

Looks like Pea's in TROUBLE.

We've gotta save him on the double, Bee!

Hooray! Bee to the rescue!

SMASH

Looks like my rescue mission needs a rescue mission . . .

ACROSS THE FARM...
Do you have any idea where he's taking us?
Not a clue!
Wonder no longer—we're there!

Oh boy. A TREE STUMP.
Wheeee.
This isn't just ANY tree stump...

Try not to POOP HONEY or JUICE YOURSELF when you see this!

It's the ULTIMATE ROLLING PARK!

I don't KNOW how to roll.
I don't even LIKE rolling.
Doesn't matter. You both get to watch ME roll!

Bee LOVED to calculate my speed and height!
Are you thinking what I'm thinking?
Yep.
WHOA!
Big air!
Jay would always cheer me on to get me PUMPED!
How did you guys like THAT action?
Guys?
Where'd you go?

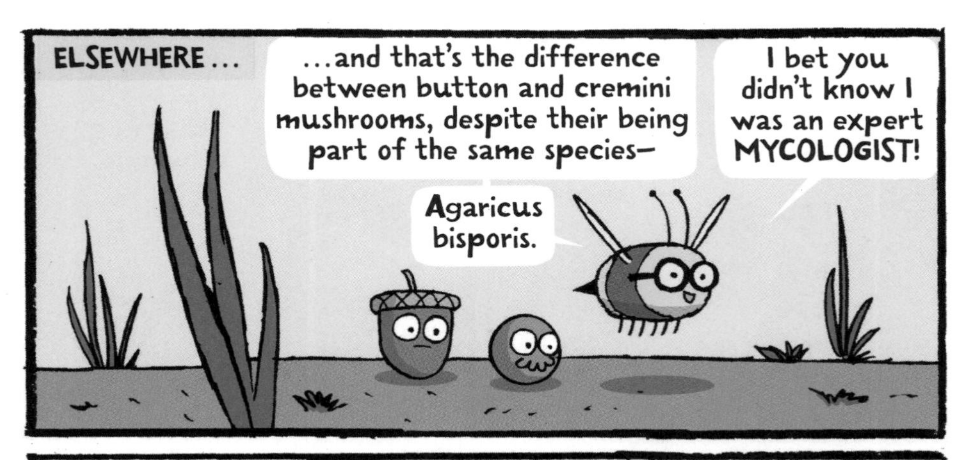
ELSEWHERE...
...and that's the difference between button and cremini mushrooms, despite their being part of the same species—
Agaricus bisporis.
I bet you didn't know I was an expert MYCOLOGIST!

Oooooh, look!
A terrestrial pulmonate gastropod mollusk.
Commonly known as a SNAIL!
Looks fishy to me.

Hold it right there, buster—you got a LICENSE to drive that SHELL?

Yes.
Looks LEGIT.

Was that really necessary?
The license checks out but that guy is DEFINITELY not telling me something.
ZZZZ

Gramps! Wake up!
BOUNCIN' BEANS!
I bet you he knows where those OTHER SUSPECTS hid their POCKETS!

I dreamed you finally stopped talking!
This whole day has been one big nightmare.
Where are the pockets, punk?!?

I'm outta here.
NO ONE HAS ANY POCKETS!
Tell Momma Pea I'm charging her DOUBLE!
Hmph! I guess I'm on my own now.
I wonder what JAY is up to...

SPEAKING OF...
Now that you two are all bandaged up, let's do some exploring!

No WAY!

Are you SEEING this?
I think that's a BIRD!

WOW WOW WOW!
Are you two FISH?
Nobody's EVER SEEN a fish before!

Pea and Bee will NEVER believe me!
You've gotta come meet my friends.
No can do. We're kinda stuck in the water.
You can join US though!

Hmm ... Pea would DEFINITELY go ...
... and Bee would want to get all of the DATA she could ...

That feels nice!
SPLISH
SPLISH

Here I go!
PLOOP

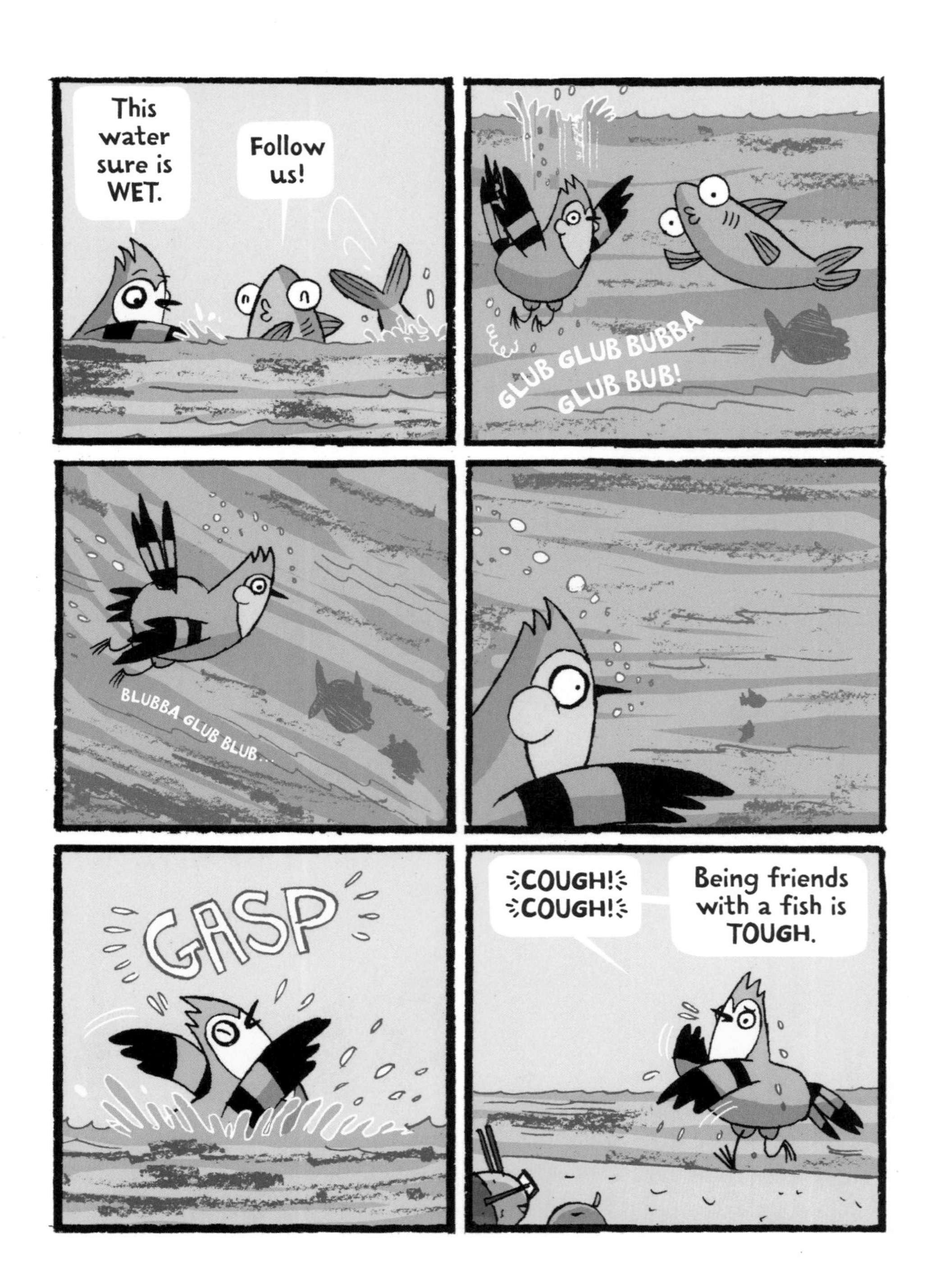
This water sure is WET.
Follow us!
GLUB GLUB BUBBA GLUB BUB!
BLUBBA GLUB BLUB...
GASP
COUGH! COUGH!
Being friends with a fish is TOUGH.

BACK ON DRY LAND...
How could those two just ditch me like that?

I can't believe they abandoned me!

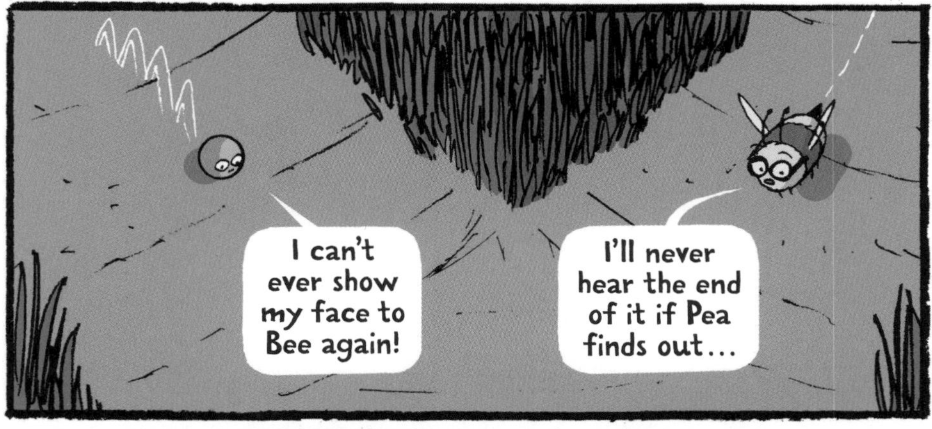
I can't ever show my face to Bee again!
I'll never hear the end of it if Pea finds out...

GASP!

I see you're all alone—what happened to your GREAT new friends?
I could ask you the same question!

Probably didn't take them long to see how STUBBORN you are.
I'M stubborn?!
YOU'RE the one who started this fight!

WHAT?!? It was you!
It was YOU and you know it!

That's Pea...
and Bee!
Sounds like they're still fighting, but at least they're TOGETHER.
GRUMBLE
GRUMBLE
GRUMBLE

Time to go to work, Jay.
I'm gonna put them back together the same way I did you two...

...whether they like it or not!

So what'd you do today that was SO COOL?
LOTS of things.
I met new mushrooms and saw a snail...
...you would have loved it!
Whoa, really?
WAITAMINNIT!
I'm still mad at you!
Actually...
...I found something pretty cool too.
I'm listening.
It's a tree stump rolling ramp!
INCREDIBLE!

Hold on
one second—
we're still
fighting!

HISSSSSSSSS

SSSSSILENCE!

You are SSSSO loud.

Tell me...what do you TASSSSTE like?
Horrible.
Absolutely TERRIBLE.

I think we should run away now.
That's the first thing we've agreed on all day.

HISSSSSSSS!

I'm too cool to get gobbled up!
Hurry—this way!

Why do you have to argue so LOUDLY?
ME?!?

Now where are they? They've gotta be around here somewhere.

YOU'RE the one with no volume control!

Oh yeah?
If we get out of this I'll show you how QUIETLY I can yell!

That doesn't make any sense at all!

Those bushes—
they're our
only chance!

Now be
quiet!

OH NO!
Pea and
Bee are in
trouble!

Do you think it saw us?
I'm too scared to run the calculations on that probability!
I can sssssssmell you...
For what it's worth I accept your apology.
I never said sorry!
RUSTLE RUSTLE
Oh! There you are!

At lassst...ssuccesss!
I am ssstarving!
CHOMP

?

PTOOEY

I ssshould have LISSSTENED...
They DO tassste AWFUL.

Wow! You TOTALLY SAVED us, Jay!
What impeccable timing!

How'd you know where to find us?
It was easy.
When you two disagree, it gets LOUD...

...very, VERY loud.
You can thank BEE for that!
Stop blaming me for what YOU did!

Can somebody PLEASE tell me what you were arguing about in the first place?
Of course! It was...
We were...

I must've...
And then...

Well, there has to be...
It was something very IMPORTANT I'm sure...

How important could it be if you can't even REMEMBER what it was?
Huh...I guess you're right!
One certainly can't argue with that logic!

I'm really sorry for everything, Bee.
Me too...

...and thank you, Jay, for showing us how silly we've been.
Best friends forever.

LATER...
Looks like there are new friendships all over the place!
How'd you like to be head of security at the hive?
I accept!

Well my name is Gramps and I'm here to say–
I love to rap in a major way!
AH BOOM POOM PIFF
AH BOOM POOM PIFF
Look! Blue finally formed his rap group!

I wonder what happened to that snake?

Tell me...what do you TASSSTE like?
Uh...
We've got to get going now.

SPLSSH

Ratsss...

Thank you to Bret Parks, Juliet Parks, Elise Parks, Robin Parks, and Ssalefish Comics, without whom this book would not have been possible.

HarperAlley is an imprint of HarperCollins Publishers.

Pea, Bee, & Jay #4: Farm Feud
Copyright © 2022 by Brian Smith
All rights reserved. Printed in Bosnia and Herzegovina.
No part of this book may be used or reproduced in any manner whatsoever without written permission except in the case of brief quotations embodied in critical articles and reviews.
For information address HarperCollins Children's Books, a division of HarperCollins Publishers, 195 Broadway, New York, NY 10007.
www.harperalley.com

Library of Congress Control Number: 2021941899
ISBN 978-0-06-298126-4 – ISBN 978-0-06-298125-7 (pbk.)

The artist used pencils, paper, a computer, and bee poop (lots and lots of bee poop) to create the digital illustrations for this book.
Typography by Erica De Chavez
21 22 23 24 25 GPS 10 9 8 7 6 5 4 3 2 1
❖
First Edition